MALPAS COURT
PRIMARY SCHOOL
WHITTLE DRIVE
MALPAS
NEWPORT
GWENT
NP9 6NS

Scholastic Children's Books,
Commonwealth House, 1-19 New Oxford Street,
London WC1A 1NU, UK
a division of Scholastic Ltd

London ~ New York ~ Toronto ~ Sydney ~ Auckland

First published by Scholastic Ltd, 1998

Developed from the original book The Night After Christmas,
by James Stephenson. The Forgotten Toys is an animated series produced
by Hibbert Ralph Entertainment for Link Entertainment,
scripted by Mark Holloway,
directed by Graham Ralph and produced by Karen Davidsen.
Executive producers David Hamilton and Claire Derry.
Script adaptation by Maria O'Neill. Book illustrations by Maureen Galvani.
All rights reserved.

2 4 6 8 10 9 7 5 3 1
ISBN 0 590 19969 2

Printed and bound in China

The Forgotten Toys

Far From Home

Summer had arrived. The toys, Annie and Teddy, were going on holiday with their children. They were inside a bag on the children's plane.

"Ow!" said Teddy.

"Are you alright?" asked Annie gently, as she took her foot out of his mouth.

"Keep your feet to yourself, Pigtails," said Teddy crossly. "I hate holidays!"

"You'll enjoy it when we get there," Annie said patiently.

The bags were unloaded and taken to the baggage hall. They went round and round on a luggage carousel waiting to be collected.

"Are we nearly there yet?" Teddy grumbled from inside the bag. "What's going on?"

"I don't know," said Annie.

"I'm going to find out," said Teddy. He scrambled up to the top of the bag and stuck his head out of the top.

"There's no one here!" he said, panicking.

"What's happened?" asked Annie, sticking her head out, too.

"Our kids – they've gone. They've forgotten us. We're lost!" Teddy wailed.

"I want to go home," said Teddy, very sadly.

"That's it!" said Annie. "We'll go home."

"We don't even know where home is," groaned Teddy.

"I do." said Annie. "It's on this label. Cheer up, Teddy, as long as we have this label we'll be fine!"

Just as she spoke, Teddy lost his balance and dropped the label. The toys gasped, as they watched the label blow away. They jumped out of the bag and ran after it.

"There it is!" cried Annie. "Come on!"

"I can't go any faster," said Teddy, trying to keep up.

Suddenly they heard a noise.

"There's someone coming," whispered Annie. "Hide!"

One of the airport cleaners walked towards them, scooped up the label and dropped it in the bin.

"Oh no!" cried Annie. Next the cleaner picked up Teddy and threw him in the bin, too!

"Pigtails! Help!" shouted Teddy.

"Teddy, can you see the label?" called Annie. Teddy tried to stand up.

"Oh, no!" he shouted.

"What?" asked Annie.

"Chewing gum! I hate chewing gum and it's all over my paw!" Teddy tried to wipe off the chewing gum and piece of paper that were stuck to his paw. "I've found the label!" he shouted. It was stuck to him!

Teddy climbed out of the bin and tumbled to the floor. But he couldn't stop! He skidded towards a woman with a suitcase. Schlooep! The chewing gum stuck to the suitcase! Annie grabbed Teddy's legs and pulled him free. But the label was gone!

"Follow that suitcase!" shouted Annie. The toys watched as the woman lifted her suitcase into the X-ray machine. Teddy crawled in after it. Annie waited.

"Teddy, where are you?" she called.

"Relax, Pigtails. I've found the label." Teddy said, happily. Just as he spoke, a man in a uniform walked past. The label stuck to his shoe. The man walked out on to the tarmac where the aeroplanes were standing. He climbed up the steps to one of the planes and went inside.

13

"We'll never get it now," said Annie. But Teddy had an idea. Nearby a small girl was carrying a huge toy panda. They were waiting in a queue to go on to the plane.

"Any chance of a lift, mate?" Teddy asked the panda.

"Si, senor," smiled the panda and lifted up his hat.

"Wheee!" shouted Teddy, as he jumped into the panda's hat.

"Any room for me?" asked Annie. The panda lifted up his poncho and Annie hid inside.

The little girl puffed and panted as she dragged her panda up the steps and on to the plane.

"Muchas gracias!" whispered Annie to the panda. She crept out from the panda's poncho and hid under one of the aeroplane seats.

The stewardess picked panda up and tidied
him away into an overhead locker.

"Pigtails!" shouted Teddy, from under
panda's hat.

But Annie wasn't listening. She saw the label, still stuck to the man's shoe, as he walked past. She crept out of her hiding place and followed him up into the cockpit. He was the pilot!

Teddy thumped on the inside of the locker. The stewardess heard the noise and opened it. Teddy came tumbling out. The stewardess caught Teddy, smiled and gave him to a baby that was crying a few seats away.

Keeping as quiet as she could, Annie crept right up to the pilot's shoe. She reached forwards to grab the label, but the pilot moved his foot and knocked her off balance.

Teddy looked up to see the stewardess closing the doors. The plane was about to take off.

Annie flew backwards and hit a lever on the control panel. Lights flashed and alarm bells rang loudly all over the plane.

"What have I done?" gasped Annie.

Everyone scrambled towards the doors.
Teddy saw Annie and grabbed her with his
sticky paw.

"We need to stick together!" shouted Teddy.
The emergency chutes opened and passengers
and toys all tumbled out of the aeroplane.

The toys sat up.

"Gosh, what an adventure!" said Annie.

"Did you get the label?" asked Teddy.

"Of course," said Annie. "Here it is."

Everything went quiet. The toys hadn't noticed everyone going back into the plane. Suddenly there was a big whoosh, as the plane took off. Annie and Teddy were lifted off their feet and blown backwards. Annie dropped the label.

They landed in a ditch, covered in rubbish.

"I hate flying! I hate holidays! I hate rubbish!" spluttered Teddy.

"Stop!" said Annie. "You've found it – the label. It's stuck to your hand!"

"Can we go home now?" asked Teddy.
"Yes. We just have to get there." said Annie.
"I'm not flying!" grumbled Teddy.
"Come on." said Annie. "We can walk."

MALPAS COURT
PRIMARY SCHOOL
WHITTLE DRIVE
MALPAS
NEWPORT
GWENT
NP9 6NS